LU

LUBBIES ARE A DANE FROM HECK

Poetry and Photos of Chiefers Barkowski

BY SHELBY MAXWELL

Copyright © 2020 Shelby Maxwell
All rights reserved.

A NOTE FROM CHIEF'S MAHM

I started writing these poems about Chief as a silly hobby to keep myself creating. Like most people and their pets, there was a distinct voice I heard in my head for him that matched his goofy personality. This made it easy to write what I figured he was thinking about when it came to everyday situations. When I started to post these on the Facebook group 'Dogspotting Society', people seemed to enjoy Chief's ridiculous views of the world as much as I enjoyed writing about them. So much so, that it wasn't long before a book, this book, was requested. As you read it, know that it is written from Chief's point of view, and that the spelling and wording reflects that fact (a term also known as "dog-speak").

I am so grateful for the people that find joy in Chief as much as I do. He has brought a love and dynamic to our family that we have never known before, and to share him with others is an absolute pleasure. I would like to say thank you to all of those people from the bottom of my heart. Without those who love Chief and his poems, none of this would be possible.

Shelby

TABLE OF CONTENTS

POEMS ABOUT CHIEF..1
   To Bork a Book 3
   No Lab in These Genes 5
   Mr. Steal Your Spot 7
   Gib Boop and Emjoy 9
   My Fren, The Sun 11
   No Take, Only Throw 13
   Come Home Soon Please 15
   Lap Machine 17
   The Cozy Squares 19
   I Jumped and Howled and Almost Peed........................21
   When I Sleep I Raise My Peet..23
   Snow 25
   Roll in the Grass 27
   Chief's Big First Birfday...29

POEMS ABOUT CADES 31
   My Cades 33
   Danger Toes 35
   Cades Do Not Cuddle 37
   Dog Bed Hogging Cade 39
   My Floof, Freddie Purrcury 41
   Shelf 43
   Best Buds 45

POEMS ABOUT HOWLIDAYS 47
   Valentime's Dane 49
   The Easter Bun 51
   Gib Thanks 53
   'Twas the Night Before Chribmus 55

CHIEF'S GUIDE TO DOG-SPEAK 56
   Dog-Speak Glossary..57

v

LUBBIES ARE A DANE FROM HECK

LUBBIES ARE A DANE FROM HECK

POEMS ABOUT CHIEF

LUBBIES ARE A DANE FROM HECK

TO BORK A BOOK

hemlo it is chief
and as you all know
i am doge poet
i rhyme like a pro

well many have said
"chief please write a book!"
so i opened one
to hab a goob look

to write a new book
did not seem so tough
i gabe it a try
i hope its enough

so here it is frens
the book is all done
ive made it happen!
it was so much fun!

i hope you emjoy
these poems of mine
i put all my lub
into every line

LUBBIES ARE A DANE FROM HECK

NO LAB IN THESE GENES

why yes, its me chief
how are you today?
im here with something
impuptant to say

the hoomans all stop
my mahm in the streets
and say "wow hes huge!
just look at those peets!"

they pat and they scritch
right behind my ears
but youll never guess
the next words i hears

"hes the biggest lab
that ive ever seen!"
heckin' wat, karen?!
no lab in these genes!

i am a great dane
a goofy lap boy
and to call me a lab
does me an annoy

LUBBIES ARE A DANE FROM HECK

LUBBIES ARE A DANE FROM HECK

MR. STEAL YOUR SPOT

my name is chief
and i steal spots
the cozy ones
you like alots

if you get up
then you can bet
ill climb right in
without much fret

i will not moves
i will not cares
ill steal your spot
most anywheres

and cuz i am
so heckin cute
you wont want to
gib me da boot

so heed my borks
or you will lose
to keep your spot
you must not moves

LUBBIES ARE A DANE FROM HECK

GIB BOOP AND EMJOY

hemlo, good day
its me, chief again
im here to ask
a favor from frens

you see dis thing?
right here, my snoot!
wouldnt you say
its so heckin cute?

so what do you do
with a snoot so cute?
well let me say frens
you gib it a boop!

no scritches, no smackies
like cade likes to do
just one smol boop?
from where? from you!

a boop tells me
im a heckin good boi
so why do you wait?
gib boop and emjoy!

LUBBIES ARE A DANE FROM HECK

MY FREN, THE SUN

my name is chief
i like the sun
its warm place is
second to none

when it does reach
the staircase top
ill walk over
and do a flop

ill do a snooze
right in its rays
no time for borks
no time for plays

and if it moves
across the floor
ill do a scooch
and snooze some more

until it sets
i cant get up
so go around
the sleepy pup

LUBBIES ARE A DANE FROM HECK

NO TAKE, ONLY THROW

hemlo its chief
am here to say
another rhyme
for you today

you see this toy?
its heckin' great
so do a throw
why do you wait?

NO HECKIN' WAY!
YOU STOP RIGHT THERE!
DONT DO A TAKE!
YOU HAB TO SHARE!

why do you try
to take the toy?
you hab to THROW
it gibs me joy!

its how we play
do you not know?
you do not take
you only throw

LUBBIES ARE A DANE FROM HECK

COME HOME SOON PLEASE

hemlo there, its chief
and im here to say
i need all your help
i am sad today

my dad left for work
so i sit and mope
my tail does not wag
my heart did a broke

my mahm heckin' tried
to cheer me back up
but nothing will work
to fix this sad pup

'til hes back from tour
i will wait right here
no walkies or lubs
could stifle these tears

if you see my dad
will you tell him from me
"good boy chief lubs you
and come home soon please"

LUBBIES ARE A DANE FROM HECK

LAP MACHINE

whats borkin' hoomans?!
im back now! hooray!
its me, your fren chief
im ready to play

my mahm works from home
on her business stuff
and when she ignores
i do a big huff

today my mahm had
her lap machine out
and wouldnt throw ball
so i did a pout

but in my tantrum
and all my appall
i figured it out!
id make her throw ball!

so i did a drop
on her dumb machine
so she'd hab to toss
my ball off her screen

dis fun game went on
it was like a dream!
but mahm figured out
my smol sneaky scheme

but dont worry frens
it all ends quite good
mahm took me outside
to play like we should

LUBBIES ARE A DANE FROM HECK

THE COZY SQUARES

hemlo its chief
and life is ruff
the cozy squares
hab lost their fluff

i dont weigh much
and though im smol
i laid my head
and crushed them all

and cuz of this
i must use three
to rest my head
and feel comfy

its not my fault
theres no more squares
for hooman heads
that i can shares

maybe my mahm
should hit the store
that sells the squares
and buy some more

LUBBIES ARE A DANE FROM HECK

I JUMPED AND HOWLED AND ALMOST PEED

hemlo its chief
its been awhile
im back to gib
you all a smile

you see dis man?
dis is my dad
and when he leebs
it makes me sad

hims plays music
with his band
he tours the world
and meets his fans

hes gone a lot
sometimes for weeks
to make da cash
to buy me treats

today my dad
came home to me
i jumped and howled
and almost peed

LUBBIES ARE A DANE FROM HECK

WHEN I SLEEP I RAISE MY PEET

my name is chief
i like to sleep
and when I do
i raise my peet

i flip myself
without a care
til my leggies
are in the air

my mahm and dad
laugh and guffaw
cuz all they see
is one lone paw

i cannot help
the way i rest
my big bed is
the heckin best

so if you want
to sleep like me
stretch out your legs
for all to see

LUBBIES ARE A DANE FROM HECK

SNOW

my name is chief
and you must know
i lub the stuff
that you call snow

in my sweater
i get all dressed
cuz snow zooms are
the heckin best

my mahm will call
and shout for me
but i wont come
am too happy

instead ill roll
and run around
all through the snow
thats on the ground

so stay warm frens!
but dont forgets
play in the snow
with no regrets

LUBBIES ARE A DANE FROM HECK

ROLL IN SOME GRASS

hemlo its me
your good fren chief
its lubly out
so ill be brief

let me show you
my favorite thing
it ends in fall
and starts in spring

the sun comes out
and does a warm
then for some months
this is the norm

the grass is soft
on my big peets
i lub it more
than good boi treats

so if you hab
a too ruff day
roll in some grass
thats what i say

LUBBIES ARE A DANE FROM HECK

CHIEF'S BIG FIRST BIRFDAY

my name is chief
and im here to say
today i am ONE
IT IS MY BIRFDAY!

my mahm did a cry
but why i dont know
she said "youre so big!
where did the time go?"

she gabe me some toys
and so many treats
we went for a walk
and had burgers to eats

she says its a day
to celebrate me
im no pup anymore
am big boi, you see!

can someone tell me
what these birfdays are?
am bamboozled frens
but i lub them so far

LUBBIES ARE A DANE FROM HECK

LUBBIES ARE A DANE FROM HECK

POEMS ABOUT CADES

LUBBIES ARE A DANE FROM HECK

MY CADES

my name is chief
i am a pup
these are my cades
wont gib them up

theyre just like me
so very smol
we nap and play
and hab a ball

and cuz i am
so heckin good
i will protecc
like goob bois should

i lub them both
dont ask me why
but theyre the best
i will not lie

so dont you dare
disturb my floofs
or you will pay
and thats the troofs

LUBBIES ARE A DANE FROM HECK

DANGER TOES

hemlo from me
your goob fren chief
i hab complaint
that brings me grief

dis is my bed
next to the warm
i lounge all day
it is the norm

today the cade
stole my big bed
and would not budge
her stoopid head

i borked and howled
and threw a fit
but this mean cade
would not move it

i am scared of
her danger toes
so please move her
and fix my woes

LUBBIES ARE A DANE FROM HECK

CADES DO NOT CUDDLE

goob morning my frens
its chief! rite on cue!
i had a weird dream
and hab to tell you

was doin a sleep
on my comfy bed
when i felt a warm
up on my big head

it was very soft
and to my surprise
it did a vibrate!
what was it you guys?!

so i took a look
but i just saw bean
she must hab scared off
that vibrate machine

why else would she be
in my bed so near
the dream makes no sense
its heckin unclear

what did you just say?
you think it was her?
cades do not cuddle!
that is just absurd!

she torments me bad
all heckin day long
she'd never cuddle
so sorry, youre wrong

LUBBIES ARE A DANE FROM HECK

DOG BED HOGGING CADE

my name is chief
as you can see
cade hogs the bed
thats meant for me

dont need much room
cuz i am smol
but she climbs up
and takes it all

i whine and cry
and do a pout
to try and get
the mean cade out

dont want to share
my comfy bed
why cant she lay
on hers instead?

if i ask nice
she will just scoff
so ill bork loud
and scare her off

LUBBIES ARE A DANE FROM HECK

MY FLOOF, FREDDIE PURRCURY

my name is chief
this is my floof
i lub himb so
it is the troof

he do a sleep
right in my bed
so i protecc
himbs tiny head

it is my job
as a good pup
wont leave my post
until hes up

if you disturb
a single hair
ill chase you off
and do a scare

so heckin shush
and do not yap
the floof is smol
and needs to nap

LUBBIES ARE A DANE FROM HECK

SHELF

my name is chief
i am a shelf
cannot get up
or move myself

the tiny cade
will climb on me
and i must lay
still as can be

for if i move
he might get scared
and danger toes
might be prepared

and if he sinks
those claws right in
ill jump and howl
and do a spin

so do not make
a single peep
to scare the cade
would make me weep

LUBBIES ARE A DANE FROM HECK

BEST BUDS

my name is chief
this is my bed
it is my spot
to rest my head

i share my bed
with the smol cade
we snuggle close
we hab it made

it brings us joy
i must inform
when mahm turns on
the wall of warm

we lub the warm
me and my floof
feels heckin nice
and thats the troof

so if youre sad
and feel like crud
just snuggle up
with your best bud

LUBBIES ARE A DANE FROM HECK

POEMS ABOUT HOWLIDAYS

LUBBIES ARE A DANE FROM HECK

VALENTIME'S DANE

hemlo it is chief
am here to explain
the valentimes day
as told by a dane

it is a whole day
for lubbies and fun
spent with your favorite
and speshul someone

it could be your cade
or hooman or pup
just pick the best one
that fills your heart up

then take that someone
and gib them some treats
tell them you lub them
and rub all their peets

but if you dont hab
someone to emjoy
do not do a fear
ill be your good boi

LUBBIES ARE A DANE FROM HECK

THE EASTER BUN

oh dear frens of mine
its me, chief the smol
and i want to gib
goob greetings to all

my mom tells me "chief!
its easter! how fun!"
i gib her this look
a bamboozled one

she said that a bun
came into our den
he left us some gifts
and snuck out again

how did i miss it?
the cute little bun
my snoot did no smells
i did not see one

i guess ill just have
to see bun in my dreams
happy easter to all
(whatever that means)

LUBBIES ARE A DANE FROM HECK

GIB THANKS

hemlo its chief
the goodest boi
here to gib thanks
and bring some joy

am thankful for
this nice warm spot
it makes me happ
a heckin lot

ill also say
am grateful for
my mahm and dad
and sibs galore

and though she does
make me afraid
am thankful for
the smol black cade

so gib a pat
or howl or rub
to gib your thanks
to those you lub

LUBBIES ARE A DANE FROM HECK

'TWAS THE NIGHT BEFORE CHRIBMUS

twas the night before chribmus and all through the den
not a chiefers was stirring, not even hims frens
the sockies were hung by the warm place with care
in the hopes that the samta paws soon would be there
the doggos were cuddled all snug in their beds
while visions of squirrels danced all in their heads
and momma in her slippers, and i with my peets,
had done goob boy tricks for a nice chimken treats,
when out on the lawn there arose such a clatter,
i sprang from my bed to see what was the matter
and what i did see sent my heart all aflutter,
was a heckin lorg sleigh and eight smol hoof puppers,
with a hooman in red driving what i saws,
i knew it right then he must be samta paws
he sprang to his sleigh and gabe the hoof pups a call
and away they all flew like freshly thrown ball
but I heard him exclaim, as he drove out of sight
"happee chribmus to all, and to all a goob night!"

CHIEF'S GUIDE TO DOG-SPEAK

As you may have noticed, Chief has a very weird vocabulary. Some words are misspelled, and others simply don't make sense at all! This is called "dog-speak". This short guide might help you to better understand exactly what Chief is trying to say in his poems.

DOG WORD	HUMAN WORD
bamboozled	confused
bork	bark
bun	bunny
cade	cat
danger toes	cat claws
doge	dog
floof	fluff/another term for a cat
frens	friends
gib	give
goob	good
happ	happy
heckin	a dog-speak "swear word"
hooman	human
lub/lubbies	love/lovies
mahm	mom
peets	paws
smol	small
snoot	nose
troof	truth

Made in the USA
Monee, IL
05 May 2020